KOALA MAKES THE RIGHT CHOICE

A book about CHOICES and CONSEQUENCES

Written by Sue Graves

Illustrated by Trevor Dunton

W

FRANKLIN WATTS
LONDON · SYDNEY

Koala didn't always make the right choices. She never looked after her bike. She always left it out in the rain. Then she got cross when it got rusty and wouldn't work.

Mum said she should make **the right choice** to look after her things.

One night, Koala didn't want to go to bed. She said she wasn't tired. Mum said she would feel **tired and grumpy** the next day.

But Koala didn't listen. She had a tantrum.
She didn't get to bed until late.

The next day, Koala was very tired.
She said she was too tired to go to school.

8

Mum said Koala should have gone to bed **on time**. She said that would have been the right choice to make.

That morning, Miss Bird read the class a story. She said everyone had to **sit quietly** and **to listen**.

YAAAWN!

But Koala **didn't sit quietly** and she **didn't listen**. Worse still, she kept yawning loudly. Miss Bird got very cross.

At painting time, Hippo broke his brush.
He asked if he could borrow Koala's.

But Koala said no even though she had finished her painting. Hippo was upset.

At lunchtime, Koala didn't choose any vegetables. Mrs Croc said vegetables were **good for you**. She said they kept you **fit and healthy**.

But Koala took no notice. She took lots of cakes instead. Tiger said cakes weren't a healthy food choice at all!

At playtime, Koala didn't make the right choices either. She didn't think about others at all. She knocked Little Lion over. She **didn't bother** to see if he was **all right**.

Everyone got cross with Koala. They said
she couldn't play with them if she didn't play
nicely. Koala was upset.

That afternoon, Koala got tummy ache.
She had to see Mr Cheetah, the school nurse.
Koala told Mr Cheetah that she had eaten
lots of cakes. Mr Cheetah said it was important
to make **the right food choices**.

Then Koala told Mr Cheetah about all her other bad choices. Mr Cheetah said that when he had to make a choice, he always remembered to **stop** and **think** first. Koala said she would try to do that, too.

That night when it was time for bed,
Koala remembered to **stop, think**
and then make the **right choice**.
Koala went to bed on time.

The next day, she didn't feel tired.
She **sat nicely** and listened to Miss Bird.

She shared her paints with Hippo and Monkey.
Hippo and Monkey said she was **very kind**.

At lunchtime, Koala remembered
to **stop**, **think** and make a **good choice**.
She chose lots of lovely vegetables.
Mrs Croc said she was **very sensible**.
Best of all, Koala didn't get tummy ache.

At playtime, Koala found a toy car
in the playground. Koala really wanted
to play with it. But it **wasn't her car**.

Koala remembered to **stop, think** and make the **right choice**. She took the car to Miss Bird. Miss Bird said the car belonged to Tiger.

Tiger was very pleased to get his car back. He asked Koala if she would like to play with him and the car. Koala was **very pleased**.

Miss Bird said Koala had made the right choice. Koala said making the right choices made her feel **much happier**.

A note about sharing this book

The *Behaviour Matters* series has been developed
to provide a starting point for further discussion on
children's behaviour both in relation to themselves
and others. The series is set in the jungle with animal
characters reflecting typical behaviour traits often seen
in young children.

Koala Makes the Right Choice
This story looks at the importance of making
the right choices in a variety of situations.

The book also reminds children that it is often a good idea to stop and
think first to give them time to make the right decision.

How to use the book
The book is designed for adults to share with either an individual child,
or a group of children, and as a starting point for discussion.

The book also provides visual support and repeated words and phrases
to build reading confidence.

Before reading the story
Choose a time to read when you and the children are relaxed and have
time to share the story.

Spend time looking at the illustrations and talk about what the book
might be about before reading it together.

Encourage children to employ a phonics first approach to tackling
new words by sounding the words out.

After reading, talk about the book with the children:

- Talk about the story with the children. Encourage them to retell the events in chronological order.

- Talk about the importance of making the right choices. Ask the children to recall incidents when they didn't make the right choice. Have they, for example, not gone to bed on time? How did they feel the next day?

- Now ask them to think about some of the choices they have made. Did they remember to sit quietly and to listen when the teacher was talking or reading a story? What did they like about making the right choice? Examples might be that they enjoyed listening to the story without any interruptions or they found it easier to do the work asked by the teacher because they had heard all the instructions.

- Take the opportunity to talk about healthy food choices. Ask their opinion on which foods are healthy and which are less so. Encourage them to talk about why good food choices are important.

- Give each child a paper plate and ask them to draw four healthy foods on it. At the end of the session, ask them to show their plates to the others and to explain their choices.

For Isabelle, William A, William G, George, Max, Emily,

Leo, Caspar, Felix, Tabitha, Phoebe and Harry –S.G.

Franklin Watts
First published in 2020 by
The Watts Publishing Group

Text © Franklin Watts 2020
Illustrations © Trevor Dunton 2020

The right of Trevor Dunton to be identified as the illustrator
of this Work has been asserted in accordance with the
Copyright, Designs and Patents Act, 1988.

Editor: Jackie Hamley
Designer: Cathryn Gilbert

A CIP catalogue record for this book is available
from the British Library.

ISBN 978 1 4451 7085 5 (hardback)
ISBN 978 1 4451 7086 2 (paperback)
ISBN 978 1 4451 8367 1 (ebook)

Printed in China

Franklin Watts
An imprint of
Hachette Children's Group
Part of The Watts Publishing Group
Carmelite House
50 Victoria Embankment
London EC4Y 0DZ

An Hachette UK company.
www.hachette.co.uk

www.hachettechildrens.co.uk

MIX
Paper from
responsible sources
FSC® C104740
FSC
www.fsc.org